HORRID HENRY

RAINY DAY DISASTER

FRANCESCA SIMON

FRANCESCA SIMON SPENT HER CHILDHOOD ON THE BEACH IN CALIFORNIA AND STARTED WRITING STORIES AT THE AGE OF EIGHT. SHE WROTE HER FIRST HORRID HENRY BOOK IN 1994. HORRID HENRY HAS GONE ON TO CONQUER THE GLOBE; HIS ADVENTURES HAVE SOLD MILLIONS OF COPIES WORLDWIDE.

FRANCESCA HAS WON THE CHILDREN'S BOOK OF THE YEAR AWARD AND IN 2009 WAS AWARDED A GOLD BLUE PETER BADGE. SHE WAS ALSO A TRUSTEE OF THE WORLD BOOK DAY CHARITY FOR SIX YEARS.

FRANCESCA LIVES IN NORTH LONDON WITH HER FAMILY.

WWW.FRANCESCASIMON.COM WWW.HORRIDHENRY.CO.UK @SIMON_FRANCESCA

TONY ROSS

TONY ROSS WAS BORN IN LONDON AND STUDIED AT THE LIVERPOOL SCHOOL OF ART AND DESIGN. HE HAS WORKED AS A CARTOONIST, A GRAPHIC DESIGNER, AN ADVERTISING ART DIRECTOR AND A UNIVERSITY LECTURER.

TONY IS ONE OF THE MOST POPULAR AND SUCCESSFUL CHILDREN'S ILLUSTRATORS OF ALL TIME, BEST KNOWN FOR ILLUSTRATING HORRID HENRY AND THE WORKS OF DAVID WALLIAMS, AS WELL AS HIS OWN HUGELY POPULAR SERIES, THE LITTLE PRINCESS. HE LIVES IN MACCLESFIELD.

HORRID HENRY
RAINY DAY DISASTER

FRANCESCA SIMON

ILLUSTRATED BY TONY ROSS

Orion

ORION CHILDREN'S BOOKS

Stories originally published in "Horrid Henry: Secret Club", "Horrid Henry: The Haunted House", "Horrid Henry: Abominable Snowman", "Horrid Henry: Rock Star", and "Horrid Henry: Zombie Vampire" respectively

This collection first published in Great Britain in 2022 by Hodder and Stoughton

1 3 5 7 9 10 8 6 4 2

Text © Francesca Simon, 1995, 1999, 2007, 2010, 2011
Illustrations © Tony Ross, 1995, 1999, 2007, 2010, 2011
Puzzles and activities © Orion Children's Books

The rights of Francesca Simon and Tony Ross to be identified as author and illustrator of this work have been asserted.

A CIP catalogue record for this book is available from the British Library.

ISBN 978 1 51010 961 2

Printed and bound in Great Britain by Clays Ltd, Elcograf S.p.a

The paper and board used in this book are from well-managed forests and other responsible sources.

MIX
Paper from responsible sources
FSC® C104740

Orion Children's Books
An imprint of
Hachette Children's Group
Part of Hodder and Stoughton
Carmelite House
50 Victoria Embankment
London EC4Y 0DZ

An Hachette UK Company
www.hachette.co.uk
www.hachettechildrens.co.uk
www.horridhenry.co.uk

CONTENTS

HORRID HENRY'S

BIRTHDAY PARTY

February was Horrid Henry's favourite month.

His birthday was in February. "**IT'S MY BIRTHDAY SOON!**" said Henry every day after Christmas. "And my birthday party! Hurray!"

February was Horrid Henry's parents' LEAST favourite month.

"It's Henry's birthday soon," said Dad, *groaning*.

"And his birthday party," said Mum, *groaning even louder*.

Every year they thought Henry's birthday parties could not get worse.

But they always did.

Every year Henry's parents said they would **NEVER EVER** let Henry have a birthday party again. But every year they gave Henry one absolutely last final chance.

Henry had BIG plans for this year's party.

"I want to go to **Lazer Zap**," said Henry. He'd been to Lazer Zap for Tough Toby's party. They'd had a great time dressing up as **spacemen** and blasting each other in dark tunnels all afternoon.

"**NO!**" said Mum. "Too violent."

"I agree," said Dad.

"And too expensive," said Mum.

"I agree," said Dad.

There was a moment's silence.

"However," said Dad, "it does mean the party wouldn't be here."

Mum looked at Dad. Dad looked at Mum.

"How do I book?" said Mum.

"**HURRAY!**" shrieked Henry.

"**Zap! Zap! Zap!**"

Horrid Henry sat in his fort holding a pad of paper. On the front cover in big capital letters Henry wrote:

HENRY'S PARTY PLANS. TOP SECRET!!!!

At the top of the first page Henry had written: **GUESTS.**

A long list followed. Then Henry stared at the names and chewed his pencil.

Actually, I don't want Margaret, thought Henry. **TOO MOODY.**

He **CROSSED** out Moody Margaret's name.

And I definitely don't want Susan. *Too crabby*.

In fact, I don't want any girls at all, thought Henry. He **CROSSED** out Clever Clare and Lazy Linda.

Then there was Anxious Andrew. **NOPE**, thought Henry, crossing him off. He's no **FUN**.

Toby was possible, but Henry didn't really like him.

Out went Tough Toby.

William?

NO WAY, thought Henry. He'll be crying the second he gets **zApped**.

Out went Weepy William.

Ralph?

Henry considered. Ralph would be good because he was sure to get into trouble. On the other hand, he hadn't invited Henry to *his* party.

Rude Ralph was **STRUCK OFF**.

So were Babbling Bob, Jolly Josh, Greedy Graham and Dizzy Dave.

And **ABSOLUTELY NO WAY** was Peter coming anywhere near him on his birthday.

Ahh, that was better. No **HORRID** kids would be coming to *his* party.

There was only one problem.

EVERY SINGLE NAME WAS CROSSED OFF.

No guests meant no presents.

Henry looked at his list. Margaret was a **moody old grouch** and he hated her, but she did sometimes give good gifts. He still had the jumbo box of **day-glo slime** she'd given him last year.

And Toby *had* invited Henry to *his* party.

And Dave was always **SPINNING** round like a top, **falling** and

knocking

things over, which was
FUN. Graham would
eat too much and burp.
And Ralph was sure
to say rude words and
make all the grown-ups angry.
Oh, let them all come,
thought Henry.
EXCEPT PETER,
of course. The
more guests I
have, the more
presents I get!

Henry turned to the next page
and wrote:

PRESENTS I WANT

SUPER SOAKER 2000, THE BEST WATER
BLASTER EVER

SPY FAX

MICRO MACHINES

SLIME

GAMEBOY

INTER-GALACTIC SAMURAI GORILLAS

STINK BOMBS

PET RATS

WHOOPEE CUSHION

25-GEAR MOUNTAIN BIKE

MONEY

He'd leave the list lying around
where Mum and Dad were sure to
find it.

"I've done the menu for the party,"
said Mum. "What do you think?"

MUM'S MENU
carrot sticks
cucumber sandwiches
peanut butter sandwiches
grapes
raisins
apple juice
carrot cake

"BLECCCCCH,"

said Henry. "I don't want that **HORRIBLE** food at my party. I want food that I like."

HENRY'S MENU

Pickled Onion Monster Munch
Smoky Spider Shreddies
Super Spicy Hedgehog Crisps
Crunchy Crackles
Twizzle Fizzle Sticks
Purple Planet-buster Drink
chocolate bars
chocolate eggs
Chocolate Monster Cake

"You can't just have **JUNK** food," said Mum.

"It's not **JUNK** food," said Henry. "Crisps are made from potatoes, and **Monster Munch** has onions — that's two vegetables."

"Henry . . ." said Mum. She looked *fierce*.

Henry looked at his menu. Then he added, in small letters at the bottom:

peanut butter sandwiches

"But **ONLY** in the middle of the table," said Henry. "So no one has to

20

eat them who doesn't want them."

"All right," said Mum. Years of fighting with Henry about his parties had worn her down.

"And Peter's not coming," said Henry.

"What?!" said Perfect Peter, looking up from polishing his shoes.

"Peter is your brother. Of course he's invited."

Henry *scowled*.

"But he'll ruin everything."

"No Peter, no party," said Mum.

Henry pretended he was a

fire-breathing dragon.

"**OWWW!**" shrieked Peter.

"Don't be **HORRID**, Henry!" yelled Mum.

"All right," said Henry. "He can come. But you'd better keep out of my way," he **hissed** at Peter.

"Mum!" wailed Peter. "Henry's being mean to me."

"Stop it, Henry," said Mum.

Henry decided to change the subject fast.

"What about **PARTY BAGS?**"
said Henry. "I want everyone to have
slime, and loads and loads and
loads of sweets! **DIRT BALLS**,
Nose Pickers and **Foam Teeth** are the
best."

"We'll see," said Mum. She looked
at the calendar. Only two more days.
Soon it would be over.

Henry's birthday arrived at last.
"HAPPY BIRTHDAY, HENRY!"
said Mum.

"**HAPPY BIRTHDAY, HENRY!**"
said Dad.

"**HAPPY BIRTHDAY, HENRY!**"
said Peter.

"Where are my **PRESENTS?**" said
Henry.

Dad pointed. Horrid Henry
ATTACKED the pile.

Mum and Dad had given him a
First Encyclopedia, **SCRABBLE**, **a
fountain pen**, a hand-knitted cardigan,
a **GLOBE**, and three sets of **VESTS
AND PANTS**.

"**OH**," said Henry. He pushed the

DREADFUL presents aside.

"Anything else?" he asked hopefully. Maybe they were keeping the **super soaker** for last.

"I've got a present for you," said Peter. "I chose it myself."

Henry tore off the wrapping paper. It was a *tapestry kit*.

"**YUCK!**" said Henry.

"I'll have it if you don't want it,"
said Peter.

"No!" said Henry, snatching up the kit.

"Wasn't it a great idea to have Henry's
party at **Lazer Zap?**" said Dad.

"Yes," said Mum. "No mess, no fuss."
They smiled at each other.

Ring ring.

Dad answered the phone. It was the
Lazer Zap lady.

"Hello! I was just ringing to check

the birthday boy's name," she said.
"We like to announce it over our
loudspeaker during the party."

Dad gave Henry's name.

A **TERRIBLE** *scream* came
from the other end of the phone. Dad
held the receiver away from his ear.

The **SHRIEKING** and
SCREAMING continued.

"Hmmmn," said Dad. "I see.
Thank you."

Dad hung up. He looked pale.

"Henry!"

"Yeah?"

27

"Is it true that you wrecked the place when you went to **Lazer Zap** with Toby?" said Dad.

"No!" said Henry. He tried to look harmless.

"And **trampled** on several children?"

"**NO!**" said Henry.

"Yes you did," said Perfect Peter.

"And what about all the **lasers** you broke?"

"What **lasers?**" said Henry.

"And the **slime** you put in the spacesuits?" said Peter.

"That wasn't me, telltale," shrieked Henry. "What about my party?"

"I'm afraid **Lazer Zap** have banned you," said Dad.

"But what about Henry's party?" said Mum. She looked pale.

"But what about my party?!" wailed Henry. "I want to go to **Lazer Zap!**"

"Never mind," said Dad brightly. "I know lots of good games."

Ding dong.

It was the first guest, Sour Susan.

She held a large present.

Henry snatched the package.

It was a pad of paper and some felt tip pens.

"How lovely," said Mum. "What do you say, Henry?"

"I've already got that," said Henry.

"Henry!" said Mum. "Don't be **HORRID!**"

I don't care, thought Henry. This

was the worst day of his life.

Ding dong.

It was the second guest, Anxious
Andrew. He held a tiny present.

Henry snatched the package.

"It's awfully small," said Henry,
tearing off the wrapping. "And it
smells."

It was a box of animal soaps.

"**HOW SUPER**," said Dad. "What
do you say, Henry?"

"**UGGHHH!**" said Henry.

"Henry!" said Dad. "Don't be horrid."

Henry stuck out his lower lip.

"It's **MY** party and I'll do what I want," muttered Henry.

"Watch your step, young man," said Dad.

Henry stuck out his tongue behind Dad's back.

More guests arrived.

Lazy Linda gave him a "Read and Listen Cassette of Favourite Fairy Tales: Cinderella, Snow White and Sleeping Beauty."

"*Fabulous*," said Mum.

"**YUCK!**" said Henry.

Clever Clare handed him a square package.

Henry held it by the corners.

"It's a book," he groaned.

"My favourite present!" said Peter.

"Wonderful," said Mum. "What is it?"

Henry unwrapped it slowly.

"Cook Your Own Healthy Nutritious Food."

"Great!" said Perfect Peter. "Can I
borrow it?"

"**NO!**" screamed Henry.

Then he threw the
book on the
floor and
stomped
on it.

"Henry!" hissed Mum. "I'm warning you. When someone gives you a present you say thank you."

Rude Ralph was the last to arrive.

He handed Henry a long rectangular package wrapped in newspaper.

It was a **Super Soaker 2000** water blaster.

"Oh," said Mum.

"Put it away," said Dad.

"Thank you, Ralph," beamed Henry. "Just what I wanted."

"Let's start with Pass the Parcel," said Dad.

"I hate Pass the Parcel," said Horrid Henry. What a **HORRIBLE** party this was.

"I love Pass the Parcel," said Perfect Peter.

"I don't want to play," said Sour Susan.

"When do we eat?" said Greedy Graham.

Dad started the music.

"Pass the parcel, William," said Dad.

"**NO!**" shrieked William. "**IT'S MINE!**"

"But the music is still playing," said Dad.

William **BURST** into tears.

Horrid Henry tried to **SNATCH** the parcel.

Dad stopped the music.

William stopped crying instantly and tore off the wrapping.

"A granola bar," he said.

"That's a **TERRIBLE** prize," said Rude Ralph.

"Is it **MY** turn yet?" said Anxious Andrew.

"When do we eat?" said Greedy Graham.

"I hate Pass the Parcel," screamed Henry. "I want to play something else."

"Musical Statues!" announced Mum brightly.

"You're out, Henry," said Dad. "You moved."

"I didn't," said Henry.

"Yes you did," said Toby.

"**NO I DIDN'T**," said Henry. "I'm not leaving."

37

"That's not fair," **SHRIEKED** Sour Susan.

"I'm not playing," whined Dizzy Dave.

"I'm tired," sulked Lazy Linda.

"I hate Musical Statues," moaned Moody Margaret.

"Where's my prize?" demanded Rude Ralph.

"A bookmark?" said Ralph. "That's it?"

"Tea time!" said Dad.

The children **PUSHED** and **shoved** their way to the table,

grabbing and snatching at the food.

"I hate **fizzy** drinks," said Tough Toby.

"I feel sick," said Greedy Graham.

"Where are the *carrot sticks?*" said Perfect Peter.

Horrid Henry sat at the head of the table.

He didn't feel like **throwing** food at Clare.

He didn't feel like **RAMPAGING** with Toby and Ralph.

He didn't even feel like **KICKING** Peter.

He wanted to be at **Lazer Zap**.

Then Henry had a wonderful, spectacular idea. He got up and sneaked out of the room.

"**PARTY BAGS**," said Dad.

"What's in them?" said Tough Toby.

"Seedlings," said Mum.

"Where are the sweets?" said Greedy Graham.

"This is the **WORST** party bag I've ever had," said Rude Ralph.

There was a noise outside.
Then Henry **BURST** into the
kitchen, **Super Soaker** in hand.

"**ZAP! ZAP! ZAP!**"

shrieked Henry, drenching everyone
with water. "Ha! Ha! Gotcha!"
Splat went the cake.
SPLASH went the drinks.

"**EEEEEEEEEEEEEEEKKK!**"

shrieked the sopping-wet children.

41

"HENRY!!!!!" yelled Mum and Dad.

"YOU **HORRID** BOY!"
yelled Mum. Water dripped from her
hair. "GO TO YOUR ROOM!"

"THIS IS YOUR LAST PARTY EVER!"
yelled Dad. Water dripped from his
clothes.

But Henry didn't care. They
said that every year.

HORRID
HENRY

AND THE COMFY
BLACK CHAIR

Ah, saturday! Best day of the week, thought Horrid Henry, flinging off the cover and leaping out of bed.

No school! No homework! A day of TV heaven! Mum and Dad liked sleeping in on a Saturday. So long as Henry and Peter were quiet they could watch TV until Mum and Dad woke up.

Horrid Henry could picture it now. He would *stretch* out in the comfy black chair, **grab** the remote control and **SWITCH** on the TV. All his favourite shows were on today: **Rapper Zapper,**

Mutant Max and Gross-Out. If he hurried he would be just in time for Rapper Zapper.

He thudded down the stairs and flung open the sitting room door. A horrible sight met his eyes.

There, stretched out on the comfy black chair and clutching the remote control, was his younger brother, Perfect Peter.

Henry gasped. How could this be?
Henry always got downstairs first.

The TV was already on. But it
was not switched to **Rapper Zapper**.
A terrible *tinkly* tune trickled out of
the TV. Oh no! It was the world's
most boring show, Daffy and her
Dancing Daisies.

"Switch the channel!" ordered
Henry. "**Rapper Zapper**'s on."

"That's a **horrid**, nasty
programme," said Perfect Peter,
shuddering. He held tight to the
remote.

"I said switch the channel!" hissed Henry.

"**I WON'T!**" said Peter. "You know the rules. The first one downstairs gets to sit in the comfy black chair and decides what to watch. And I want to watch Daffy."

Henry could hardly believe his ears. Perfect Peter was . . . refusing to obey an order?

"**NO!**" screamed Henry. "I hate that show. I want to watch Rapper Zapper!"

"Well, I want to watch Daffy," said Perfect Peter.

"But that's a baby show," said Henry.

"*Dance, my daisies, dance!*" squealed the revolting Daffy.

"La, la la la la!" trilled the daisies.

"La, la la la la!" sang Peter.

"Baby, baby!" taunted Henry. If only he could get Peter to run upstairs crying then *he* could get the chair.

"**Peter is a baby, Peter is a baby!**" jeered Henry.

Peter kept his eyes glued to the screen.

Horrid Henry could stand it no longer. He *pounced* on Peter, **SNATCHED**

the remote and **pushed** Peter on
to the floor. He was **Rapper Zapper**
liquidating a pesky android.

"**AAAAAH**!" screamed Perfect Peter.
"MUUUMMM!"

Horrid Henry leapt into the comfy
black chair and switched channels.

"Grrrrrrr!" growled
Rapper Zapper,

blasting a baddie.

"**DON'T BE HORRID, HENRY!**"
shouted Mum, storming through the
door. "**GO TO YOUR ROOM!**"

"NOOOO!" wailed Henry. "Peter
started it!"

"**NOW!**" screamed Mum.

"La, la la la la!" trilled the daisies.

BUZZZZZZZZZ.
Horrid Henry switched off the
alarm. It was six a.m. the following

Saturday. Henry was taking no chances. Even if he had to grit his teeth and watch **Rise and Shine** before **Gross-Out** started it was worth it. And he'd seen the coming attractions for today's **Gross-Out**: who could eat the most cherry pie in five minutes while blasting the other contestants with a **Goo-Shooter**. Henry couldn't wait.

There was no sound from Peter's room. Ha, ha, thought Henry. He'll have to sit on the lumpy sofa and watch what *I* want to watch.

Horrid Henry skipped into the sitting room. And stopped.

"Remember, children, always eat with a knife and fork!" beamed a cheerful presenter. It was *Manners with Maggie*. There was Perfect Peter in his slippers and dressing gown, stretched out on the comfy black chair. Horrid Henry felt sick. Another Saturday ruined!

He had to watch **Gross-Out!** He just had to.

Horrid Henry was just about to push Peter off the chair when he stopped. Suddenly he had a *brilliant* idea.

"Peter! Mum and Dad want to see you. They said it's urgent!"

Perfect Peter leapt off the comfy black chair and dashed upstairs.

Tee hee, thought Horrid Henry.

ZAP!

"Welcome to *Gross-Out!*" shrieked the presenter, Marvin the Maniac. "Boy, will you all be feeling sick today! It's *Gross! Gross! Gross!*"

"Yeah!" said Horrid Henry. This was great!

Perfect Peter reappeared.

"They didn't want me," said Peter. "And they're CROSS because I woke them up."

"They told me they did," said Henry, eyes glued to the screen.

Peter stood still.

"Please give me the chair back, Henry."

Henry didn't answer.

"I had it first," said Peter.

"Shut up, I'm trying to watch," said Henry.

"**EWWWWWW, GROSS!**" screamed the TV audience.

"I was watching *Manners with Maggie*," said Peter. "She's showing how to eat soup without slurping."

"Tough," said Henry. "Oh, **gross!**" he chortled, pointing at the screen.

Peter hid his eyes.

"**Muuuuummmmmmmm!**" shouted Peter. "Henry's being **mean** to me!"

Mum appeared in the doorway. She looked furious.

"**HENRY, GO TO YOUR ROOM!**" shouted Mum. "We were

trying to sleep. Is it too much to ask to be left in peace one morning a week?"

"But Peter—"

Mum pointed to the door.

"Out!" said Mum.

"**IT'S NOT FAIR!**" howled Henry, stomping off.

ZAP!

"And now Kate, our guest manners expert, will demonstrate the proper way to butter toast."

Henry *slammed* the door behind him as hard as he could. Peter had

got the comfy black chair for the
very last time.

BUZZZZZZZZZ.

Horrid Henry switched off
the alarm. It was two a.m. the

following Saturday. The **Gross-Out** Championships were on in the morning. He **grabbed** his pillow and duvet and sneaked out of the room. He was taking no chances. Tonight he would *sleep* in the comfy black chair. After all, Mum and Dad had never said how *early* he could get up.

Henry tiptoed out of his room into the hall.

All quiet in Peter's room.

All quiet in Mum and Dad's.

Henry crept down the stairs and carefully opened the sitting room door.

The room was **pitch black**. Better not turn on the light, thought Henry. He felt his way along the wall until his fingers touched the back of the comfy black chair. He felt around the top. Ah, there was the remote. He'd sleep with that under his pillow, just to be safe.

Henry flung himself on to the chair and landed on something lumpy.

"**AHHHHHHHHH!**" screamed Henry.

"**AHHHHHHHHH!**" screamed the Lump.

"**HELP!**" screamed Henry and the Lump.

Feet pounded down the stairs.

"What's going on down there?"
shouted Dad, switching on the light.

Henry blinked.

"Henry jumped on my head!"
snivelled a familiar voice beneath
him.

"*Henry, what are you doing?*" said Dad. "It's two o'clock in the morning!"

Henry's brain whirled. "I thought I heard a burglar so I crept down to keep watch."

"Henry's lying!" said Peter, sitting up. "He came down because he wanted the comfy black chair."

"**LIAR!**" said Henry. "And what were *you* doing down here?"

"I couldn't sleep and I didn't want to wake you, Dad," said Peter. "So I came down as quietly as I could to get a drink of water. Then I felt sleepy and lay down for a moment. I'm very sorry, Dad, it will never happen again."

"All right," said Dad, stifling a yawn. "From now on, you are not to come down here before seven a.m. or there will be *no TV for a week!* Is that clear?"

"Yes, Dad," said Peter.

"Yeah," muttered Henry.

He glared at Perfect Peter.

Perfect Peter glared at Horrid Henry. Then they both went upstairs to their bedrooms and closed the doors.

"GOODNIGHT!" called Henry cheerfully. "My, I'm sleepy."

But Henry did not go to bed. He needed to think.

He *could* wait until everyone was asleep and sneak back down. But what if he got caught? No TV for a week would be UNBEARABLE.

But what if he missed the **Gross-Out** Championships? And never found out if Tank Thomas or Tapioca Tina won the day? Henry shuddered. There had to be a better way.

Ahh! He had it! He would set his clock ahead and make sure he was first down. Brilliant! **Gross-Out** here I come, he thought.

But wait. What if Peter had the *same* **brilliant** idea? That would spoil everything. Henry had to double-check.

Henry opened his bedroom door.
The coast was clear. He tiptoed out and
SNEAKED into Peter's room.

There was Peter, sound asleep. And
there was his clock. Peter hadn't
changed the time. Phew.

And then Henry had a truly
WICKED idea. It was so evil, and
so horrid, that for a moment even
he hesitated. But hadn't Peter been
horrible and SELFISH, stopping Henry
watching his favourite shows? He
certainly had. And wouldn't it be great
if Peter got into trouble, just for once?

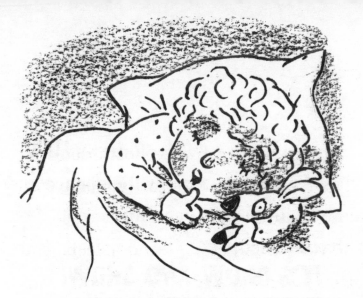

Perfect Peter rolled over. "La, la la la la," he warbled in his sleep.

That did it. Horrid Henry moved Peter's clock an hour ahead. Then Henry sneaked downstairs and

turned up the TV's volume as **LOUD** as it would go. Finally, he opened Mum and Dad's door, and crept back to bed.

"IT'S GROW AND SHOW! THE VEGETABLE SHOW FOR TINIES! JUST LOOK AT ALL THESE LOVELY VEGETABLES!"

The terrible noise **BOOMED** through the house, blasting Henry out of bed.

"HENRY!" bellowed Dad. "Come here this instant!"

Henry sauntered into his parents'
bedroom.

"What is it?" he asked, yawning
loudly.

Mum and Dad looked confused.

"Wasn't that you watching TV
downstairs?"

"No," said Henry, stretching. "I was
asleep."

Mum looked at Dad.

Dad looked at Mum.

"You mean Peter is downstairs
watching TV at six a.m.?"

Henry shrugged.

"Send Peter up here this minute!"
said Dad.

For once Henry did not need to be
asked twice. He ran downstairs and
BURST into the sitting room.

"I GREW CARROTS!"
"I GREW STRING BEANS!"

"Peter! Mum and Dad want to see
you right away!" said Henry.

Peter didn't look away from Grow
and Show.

"PETER! Dad asked me to send you up!"

"You're just trying to trick me," said
Peter.

"You'd better go or you'll be in **big** trouble," said Henry.

"Fool me once, shame on you. Fool me twice, shame on me," said Peter. "I'm not moving."

"Now, just look at all these beautiful tomatoes Timmy's grown," squealed the TV.

"Wow," said Peter.

"Don't say I didn't warn you," said Henry.

"**PETER!**" bellowed Dad. "**NO TV FOR A MONTH! COME HERE THIS MINUTE!**"

Perfect Peter burst into tears. He jumped from the chair and crept out of the room.

Horrid Henry sauntered over to the comfy black chair and stretched out. He picked up the remote and switched channels.

ZAP!

Rapper Zapper stormed into the spaceship and pulverised some alien slime.

"Way to go, Rapper Zapper!" shrieked Horrid Henry. Soon Gross-Out would be on. wasn't life sweet?

HORRID HENRY'S

RAINY DAY

Horrid Henry was bored.
Horrid Henry was fed up.

He'd been **BANNED** from the computer for rampaging through Our Town Museum. He'd been **BANNED** from watching TV just because he was caught watching a TEENY TINY bit extra after he'd been told to switch it off straight after **Mutant Max**. Could he help it if an exciting new series about a rebel robot had started right after? How would he know if it were any good unless he watched some of it?

It was completely unfair and all

Peter's fault for telling on him, and Mum and Dad were the MEANEST, most horrible parents in the world.

And now he was stuck indoors, all day long, with absolutely NOTHING to do.

The rain splattered down. The house was grey. The world was grey. The universe was grey.

"I'M BORED!" wailed Horrid Henry.

"Read a book," said Mum.

"Do your homework," said Dad.

"NO!" said Horrid Henry.

"Then tidy your room," said Mum.

"Unload the dishwasher," said Dad.

"Empty the bins," said Mum.

"**NO WAY!**" shrieked Horrid Henry. What was he, a **BUTLER?** Better keep out of his parents' way, or they'd come up with even more **horrible** things for him to do.

Horrid Henry stomped up to his boring bedroom and *slammed* the door. **UGGH.** He **HATED** all his toys. He **HATED** all his music. He **HATED** all his games. **UGGGHHHHHH!**

What could he do?

Aha.

He could always check to see what Peter was up to.

Perfect Peter was sitting in his room arranging stamps in his stamp album.

"Peter is a baby, Peter is a baby," jeered **Horrid Henry**, sticking his head round the door.

"Don't call me *baby*," said Perfect
Peter.

"Okay, **Duke of Poop**," said Henry.

"Don't call me **Duke**!" shrieked Peter.

"Okay, *Poopsicle*," said Henry.

"MUUUUM!" wailed Peter. "Henry
called me *Poopsicle*!"

"Don't be **HORRID**, Henry!" shouted
Mum. "Stop calling your brother
names."

Horrid Henry smiled sweetly at
Peter.

"Okay, Peter, 'cause I'm so *nice*,
I'll let you make a list of ten names

that you don't want to be called," said
Henry. "And it will only cost you £1."

£1! Perfect Peter could not believe
his ears. Peter would pay much more
than that never to be called Poopsicle
again.

"Is this a trick, Henry?" said Peter.

"No," said Henry. "How dare you?
I make you a good offer, and you
accuse me. Well, just for that—"

"Wait," said Peter. "I accept." He
handed Henry a pound coin. At last,
all those HORRID names would be
banned. Henry would never call him

Duke of Poop again.

Peter got out a piece of paper and a pencil.

Now, let's see, what to put on the list? thought Peter. Poopsicle, for a start. And I hate being called Baby, and **Nappy Face**, and **Duke of Poop**.

Peter wrote and wrote and wrote.

"Okay, Henry, here's the list," said Peter.

NAMES I DON'T WANT
TO BE CALLED

1. Poopsicle
2. Duke of Poop
3. Ugly
4. Nappyface
5. Baby
6 Toad
7. Smelly toad
8. Ugg
9. Worm
10. Wibble pants

Horrid Henry scanned the list.
"Fine, PONGY PANTS," said Henry.
"Sorry, I meant **poopy pants**. Or was it
SMELLY NAPPY?"

"MUUUMM!" wailed Peter. "Henry's
calling me names!"

"**HENRY!**" screamed Mum. "For
the last time, can't you leave your
brother alone?"

Horrid Henry considered. Could he
leave that *worm* alone?

"**Peter is a frog,
Peter is a frog**,"
chanted Henry.

"MUUUUUMMMMM!" screamed Peter.

"That's it, Henry!" shouted Mum. "No **POCKET MONEY** for a week. Go to your room and stay there."

"**FINE!**" shrieked Henry. "You'll all be sorry when I'm **DEAD**." He **STOMPED** down the hall and *slammed* his bedroom door as hard as he could. Why were his parents so **mean** and **HORRIBLE**? He was hardly bothering Peter at all. Peter **WAS** a frog. Henry was only telling the truth.

Boy, would they be sorry when he'd died of boredom stuck up here.

If only we'd let him watch
a little extra **TV**, Mum
would wail. Would
that have been so
TERRIBLE?

If only we hadn't
made him do any
chores, Dad would
sob.

Why didn't I let
Henry call me
names, Peter would
howl. After all, I do
have *smelly pants*.

And now it's too late and we're SOOOOOOO SORRY, they would shriek.

But wait. Would they be sorry? Peter would *grab* Henry's room. And all his best toys. His arch-enemy STUCK-UP STEVE could come over and snatch anything he wanted, even his skeleton bank and **Goo-Shooter**. Peter could invade the PURPLE HAND FORT and Henry couldn't stop him. Moody Margaret could hop over the wall and nick his flag. And his biscuits. And his Dungeon Drink Kit. Even his . . . SUPER SOAKER.

NOOOOOO!!!

Horrid Henry went pale. He had
to stop those rapacious thieves.
But how?

I could come back and **haunt** them,
thought Horrid Henry. Yes! That
would teach those grave-robbers

not to mess with me.

"**Oooooooo, get out of my roooooooooooom, you horrrrrrrible toooooooooooooad**," he would moan at Peter.

"Touch my **Gooooooooo-shoooooooter** and you'll be *morphed* into **ectoplasm**," he'd groan spookily from under STUCK-UP STEVE'S bed. Ha! That would show him.

Or he'd pop out from inside MOODY MARGARET'S wardrobe.

"**Giiiiive Henrrrrry's toyyyys**

back, you mis-er-a-ble sliiiiiimy snake," he would rasp. That would teach her a thing or two.

Henry smiled. But fun as it would be to haunt people, he'd rather stop horrible enemies **SNATCHING** his stuff in the first place.

And then suddenly **Horrid Henry**

had a brilliant, SPECTACULAR idea. Hadn't Mum told him just the other day that people wrote wills to say who they wanted to get all their stuff when they died? Henry had been thrilled.

"So when you die I get all your money!" Henry beamed. WOW. The HOUSE would be his! And the CAR! And he'd be boss of the TV, 'cause it would be his, too! And the only shame was—

"Couldn't you just give it all to me now?" asked Henry.

"**HENRY!**" snapped Mum. "Don't be **HORRID**."

There was no time to lose. He had to write a will immediately.

Horrid Henry sat down at his desk and grabbed some paper.

MY WILL
WARNING: DO NOT READ UNLESS
I AM DEAD!!!! I mean it!!!!

If you're reading this it's because I'm dead and you aren't. I wish you were dead and I wasn't, so I could have all your stuff. It's so not fair.

First of all, to anyone thinking of snatching my stuff just 'cause I'm dead . . .

BEWARE! Anyone who doesn't do what I say will get haunted by a bloodless and boneless ghoul, namely me. So there.

Now the hard bit, thought Horrid Henry. Who should get his things? Was anyone deserving enough?

Peter, you are a worm. And a toad. And an ugly baby nappy face smelly ugg wibble pants poopsicle. I leave you . . .

Hmmmn.

That **toad** really shouldn't get anything. But Peter was his brother after all.

I leave you my sweet wrappers.

And a muddy twig.

That was more than Peter deserved. Still . . .

Steve, you are stuck-up and horrible and the world's worst cousin. You can have a pair of my socks. You can choose the blue ones with the holes or the falling down orange ones.

Margaret, you nit-face. I give you the Purple

Hand flag to remember me by— NOT! You can have two radishes and the knight with the chopped-off head. And keep your paws off my Grisly Grub Box!!! Or else . . .

Miss Battle-Axe, you are my worst teacher ever. I leave you a broken pencil.

Aunt Ruby, you can have the lime green cardigan back that you gave me for Christmas.

Hmmm. So far he wasn't doing so well giving away any of his good things.

Ralph, you can have my Goo-Shooter, but ONLY if you give me your football and your bike and your computer game Slime Ghouls.

That was more like it. After all, why should he be the only one writing a will? It was certainly a lot more fun thinking about getting stuff from other people than giving away his own *treasures*.

In fact, wouldn't he be better off helping others by telling them what he wanted? Wouldn't it be AWFUL if Rich Aunt Ruby left him some of Steve's old clothes in her will

thinking that he would be delighted?

Better write to her at once.

Dear Aunt Ruby
I am leeving you
Something ~~geet REELY~~
~~GREAT~~ REELY
REELY GREAT in
my will, so make sure
you leeve me loads of
Cash in yours.
    Your favorite nephew
        Henry

Now, Steve. Henry was leaving him an **old pair of holey socks**. But Steve didn't have to know that, did he. For all Henry knew, Steve **LOVED** holey socks.

Dear Steve

You know your new
blue racing bike
with the silver trim?
Well when your dead
it wont be any use to you,
so please leave it to me
in your will
                Your favourite cousin
                        Henry
P.S By the way,
no need to wait till your dead,
you can give it to me now.

Right, Mum and Dad. When they were in the old people's home they'd hardly need a thing. A *rocking chair* and *blanket* each would do fine for them.

So, how would Dad's *music system* look in his bedroom? And where could he put Mum's **CLOCK RADIO**? Henry had always liked the *chiming*

clock on their mantelpiece and the picture of the blackbird. Better go and check to see where he could put them.

Henry went into Mum and Dad's room, and *grabbed* an armload of stuff. He **staggered** to his bedroom and **DUMPED** everything on the floor, then went back for a second helping. **Stumbling** and **staggering**

under his heavy burden, Horrid Henry *swayed* down the hall and **CRASHED** into Dad.

"What are you doing?" said Dad, staring. "That's mine."

"And those are mine," said Mum. **"WHAT IS GOING ON?"** shrieked Mum and Dad.

"I was just checking how all this stuff will look in my room when you're in the old people's home," said **Horrid Henry**.

"I'm not there yet," said Mum.

"Put **EVERYTHING** back," said Dad.

Horrid Henry **SCOWLED**. Here he was, just trying to think ahead, and he gets told off.

"Well, just for that I **WON'T** leave you **ANY** of my knights in my will," said Henry.

Honestly, some people were so selfish.

HORRID HENRY'S

INVASION

Peter

"BAA! BAA! BAA!"

Perfect Peter baaed happily at his sheep collection. There they were, his ten lovely little *sheepies*, all beautifully lined up from **biggest** to SMALLEST, heads facing forward, fluffy tails against the wall, all five centimetres apart from one another, all—

Perfect Peter gasped. Something was wrong. Something was **TERRIBLY** wrong. But what? What? Peter scanned the mantelpiece. Then he saw . . .

NOoOOo!

FLUFF PUFF, his favourite sheep, the one with the pink and yellow nose, was facing the wrong way round. His nose was **shoved** against the wall. His tail was facing forward. And he was . . . he was . . . **crooked!**

This could only mean . . . this could only mean . . .

"Mum!" screamed Peter. "Mum! Henry's been in my room again!"

"**HENRY!**" shouted Mum. "Keep out of Peter's room."

"**I'm not in Peter's room**," yelled **Horrid Henry**. "I'm in mine."

"But he was," wailed Peter.

"Wasn't!" bellowed Horrid Henry.

Tee hee.

Horrid Henry was strictly forbidden to go into Peter's bedroom without **Peter's** permission. But sometimes, thought Horrid Henry, when Peter was being even more of a **toady toad** than usual, he had no choice but to invade.

Peter had run blabbing to Mum that Henry had watched **Mutant Max** and **Knight Fight** when Mum had said he could only watch one or the other. Henry had been banned from watching TV all day. Peter was such a *telltale* **frogface** ninnyhammer **toady** POO BAG, thought Horrid Henry grimly. Well, just wait till Peter tried to colour in his new picture, he'd—

"MUM!" screamed Peter. "Henry switched the caps on my coloured pens. I just put pink in the sky."

"DIDN'T!" yelled Henry.

"Did!" wailed Peter.

"Prove it," said Horrid Henry, smirking.

Mum came upstairs. Quickly Henry

leapt over the mess covering the floor of his room, **flopped** on his bed and grabbed a **Screamin' Demon** comic. Peter came and stood in the doorway.

"Henry's being **HORRID**," snivelled Peter.

"Henry, have you been in Peter's room?" said Mum.

Henry sighed loudly. "Of course I've been in his **smelly** room. I live here, don't I?"

"I mean when he wasn't there," said Mum.

"No," said Horrid Henry. This wasn't a lie, because even if Peter wasn't there his **HORRIBLE** stinky smell was.

"He has too," said Peter. "**FLUFF PUFF** was turned the wrong way round."

"Maybe he was just trying to escape from your **pongy pants**," said Henry. "I would."

"Mum!" said Peter.

"Henry! Don't be **HORRID**. Leave your brother alone."

"I am leaving him alone," said Horrid Henry. "Why can't he leave me alone? And get out of my room, Peter!" he shrieked as Peter put his foot just inside Henry's door.

Peter quickly withdrew his foot.

Henry *glared* at Peter.

Peter *glared* at Henry.

Mum sighed. "The next one who goes into the other's room without permission will be banned from the

COMPUTER for a week. And no
pocket money either."

She turned to go.

Henry stuck out his tongue at Peter.

"Telltale," he mouthed.

"Mum!" screamed Peter.

Perfect Peter stalked back to his
bedroom. How dare Henry sneak
in and mess up his sheep? What a
MEAN, HORRIBLE brother. Perhaps
he needed to calm down and listen
to a little music. The Daffy and her

Dancing Daisies Greatest Hits CD
always cheered him up.

> "Dance and prance.
> Prance and dance.
> You say moo moo. We say baa.
> Everybody says moo moo baa baa,"

piped Perfect Peter as he put on the
Daffy CD.

"BOILS ON YOUR FAT FACE
BOILS MAKE YOU DUMB.
CHOP CHOP CHOP 'EM OFF
STICK 'EM ON YOUR BUM!"

blared the CD player.

Huh? What was that **HORRIBLE** song? Peter yanked out the CD. It was the **Skullbangers** singing the horrible "**BONY BOIL**" song. Henry must have sneaked a **Skullbanger** CD inside the Daffy case. How dare he? How dare he? Peter would storm straight downstairs and tell Mum. Henry would get into big trouble. **BIG BIG TROUBLE**.

Then Peter paused. There was the TEENY-TINY possibility that Peter had mixed them up by mistake . . . No. He needed absolute proof of

Henry's **HORRIDNESS**. He'd do his
homework, then have a good look
around Henry's room to see if his
Daffy CD was hidden there.

Peter glanced at his "To Do" list,
pinned on his noticeboard. When he'd
written it that morning it read:

Peter's To Do List
Practise cello
Fold clothes and put away
Do homework
Brush my teeth
Read Bunny's Big Boo Boo

The list now read:

Peter's To Do List
Practise ~~cello~~ belly dancing
~~un~~Fold clothes and ~~Put~~ away throw
~~Don't do~~ homework
~~F~~lush my teeth ~~down the toilet~~
Read Bunny's Big ~~Poo Poo~~

At the bottom someone had added:

Pick my nose
Pinch mum
Give Henry all my money

120

Well, here was proof! He was going to go straight down and tell on Henry.

"Mum! Henry's been in my room again. He scribbled all over my To Do list."

"**HENRY!**" screamed Mum. "I am sick and tired of this! Keep out of your brother's bedroom! This is your last warning! No playing on the computer for a week!"

SNEAK. SNEAK. SNEAK.

Horrid Henry slipped inside

the enemy's bedroom. He'd pay Peter back for getting him banned from the computer.

There was Peter's cello. **HA!** It was the work of a moment to unwind all the strings. Now, what else, what else? He could *switch* around Peter's pants and sock drawers.

NO! Even better. Quickly Henry undid all of Peter's socks, and mismatched them. Who said socks should match?

TEE HEE. Peter would go **MAD** when he found out he was wearing one

Sammy the Snail sock with one **Daffy** sock. Then Henry snatched **BUNNYKINS** off Peter's bed and crept out.

SNEAK. SNEAK. SNEAK.

Perfect Peter crept down the hall and stood outside Henry's bedroom, holding a **MUDDY TWIG**. His heart was **POUNDING**. Peter knew he was strictly forbidden to go into Henry's room without permission. But Henry kept

breaking that rule. So why shouldn't he?

Squaring his shoulders, Peter tiptoed in.

Crunch.
Crunch.
Crunch.

Henry's room was a pigsty, thought Perfect Peter, wading through broken knights, crumpled sweet wrappers, dirty clothes, ripped comics and muddy shoes.

Mr Kill. He'd steal Mr Kill. HA!

Serve Henry right. And he'd put the
MUDDY TWIG in Henry's bed. Serve him
double right. Perfect Peter **grabbed**
Mr Kill, shoved the twig in Henry's
bed and nipped back to his room.

And SCREAMED.

FLUFF PUFF wasn't just turned
the wrong way, he was — GONE!

Henry must have stolen him. And Lambykins was gone too. And Squish. Peter only had seven sheep left.

And where was his BUNNYKINS? He wasn't on the bed where he belonged. No!!!!!! This was the last straw. This was war.

The coast was clear. Peter always took ages having his bath. Horrid Henry slipped into the worm's room.

He'd pay Peter back for stealing Mr Kill. There he was, shoved at

the top of Peter's wardrobe, where
Peter always hid things he didn't
want Henry to find. Well, **HA HA HA**,
thought Horrid Henry, rescuing
Mr Kill.

Now what to do, what to do? Horrid
Henry *scooped* up all of Peter's
remaining sheep and **shoved** them
inside Peter's pillowcase.

What else? Henry glanced round Peter's immaculate room. He could mess it up. Nah, thought Henry. Peter loved tidying. He could — aha.

Peter had pinned drawings all over the wall above his bed. Henry surveyed them. Shame, thought Henry, that Peter's pictures were all so dull. I mean, really, "My Family", and "MY BUNNYKINS". Horrid Henry climbed on Peter's bed to reach the drawings.

Poor Peter, thought Horrid Henry. What a TERRIBLE artist he was. No

wonder he was such a *smelly toad* if he had to look at such **AWFUL** pictures all the time. Perhaps Henry could improve them . . .

Now, let's see, thought **Horrid Henry**, getting out some crayons. Drawing a crown on my head would be a big improvement. There! That livens things up. And a **BIG RED NOSE** on Peter would help, too, thought Henry, drawing away. So would a **droopy** moustache on Mum. And as for that stupid picture of **BUNNYKINS**, well, why not draw

a lovely toilet for him to—

"What are you doing in here?" came a little voice.

Horrid Henry turned.

There was Peter, in his *bunny pyjamas*, glaring at him.

Uh oh. If Peter told on him again, Henry would be in **BIG, BIG, MEGA-BIG TROUBLE**. Mum would probably ban him from the **COMPUTER** for ever.

"You're in my room. I'm telling on you," shrieked Peter.

"Shhh!" hissed Horrid Henry.

"What do you mean, shhh?" said

Peter. "I'm going straight down to tell Mum."

"One word and you're **DEAD**, worm," said Horrid Henry. "Quick! Close the door."

Perfect Peter looked behind him. "Why?"

"Just do it, *worm*," hissed Henry.

Perfect Peter shut the door.

"What are you doing?" he demanded.

"Dusting for fingerprints," said Horrid Henry *smoothly*.

Fingerprints?

"What?" said Peter.

"I thought I heard someone in your room, and ran in to check you were okay. Just look what I found," said Horrid Henry dramatically, pointing to Peter's now empty mantelpiece.

Peter let out a squeal.

"My sheepies!" wailed Peter.

"I think there's a burglar in the house," whispered Horrid Henry urgently. "And I think he's hiding . . .

in your room."

Peter gulped. A burglar? In his room?

"A burglar?"

"Too right," said Henry. "Who do you think stole BUNNYKINS? And all your sheep?"

"You," said Peter.

Horrid Henry snorted. "No! What would I want with your STUPID sheep? But a sheep rustler would love them."

Perfect Peter hesitated. Could Henry be telling the truth? Could a burglar really have stolen his sheep?

"I think he's hiding under the bed," hissed Horrid Henry. "Why don't you check?"

Peter stepped back.

"No," said Peter. "I'm scared."

"Then get out of here as quick as you can," whispered Henry. "I'll check."

"Thank you, Henry," said Peter.

Perfect Peter crept into the hallway. Then he stopped. Something wasn't right . . . something was a little bit wrong.

Perfect Peter **MARCHED** back into his bedroom. Henry was by the door.

"I think the burglar is hiding in your wardrobe, I'll get—"

"You said you were fingerprinting," said Peter suspiciously. "With what?"

"My fingers," said Horrid Henry. "Why do you think it's called fingerprinting?"

Then Peter caught sight of his drawings.

"You've **RUINED** my pictures!"

shrieked Peter.

"It wasn't me, it must have been the burglar," said Horrid Henry.

"You're trying to **trick** me," said Peter. "I'm telling!"

Time for Plan B.

"I'm only in here 'cause you were in my room," said Henry.

"Wasn't!"

"Were!"

"Liar!"

"Liar!"

"You stole BUNNYKINS!"

"You stole Mr Kill!"

"Thief!"

"Thief!"

"I'm telling on you."

"I'm telling on you!"

Henry and Peter *glared* at each other.

"**Okay**," said **Horrid Henry**. "I won't invade your room if you won't invade mine."

"Okay," said Perfect Peter. He'd agree to anything to get Henry to leave his sheep alone.

Horrid Henry smirked.

He couldn't wait until tomorrow when Peter tried to play his cello . . . tee hee. Wouldn't he get a shock!

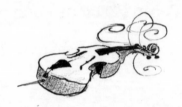

MOODY MARGARET'S
SLEEPOVER

"What are you doing here?" said Moody Margaret, glaring.

"I'm here for the sleepover," said Sour Susan, glaring back.

"You were uninvited, remember?" said Margaret.

"And then you invited me again, remember?" snapped Susan.

"**Did not**."

"Did too. You told me last week I could come."

"Didn't."

"Did. You're such a MEANIE, Margaret," scowled Susan.

AAAARRGGGHH. Why was she friends with such a **MOODY OLD GROUCH?**

MOODY MARGARET heaved a heavy sigh. Why was she friends with such a sour old *slop bucket*?

"Well, since you're here, I guess you'd better come in," said Margaret. "But don't expect any dessert 'cause there won't be enough for you and my real guests."

Sour Susan *stomped* inside Margaret's house. Grrrr. She wouldn't be inviting Margaret to her next sleepover party, that's for sure.

Horrid Henry couldn't sleep. He was hot. He was hungry.

"Biscuits!" moaned his tummy. "Give me biscuits!"

Because Mum and Dad were the **MEANEST**, most **HORRIBLE** parents in the world, they'd forgotten to buy more biscuits and there wasn't a SINGLE SOLITARY CRUMB in the house. Henry knew because he'd searched everywhere.

"**GIVE ME BISCUITS!**" growled his tummy. "What are you waiting for?"

I'm going to die of hunger up here, thought **Horrid Henry**. And it will be all Mum and Dad's fault. They'll come in tomorrow morning and find just a few WISPS of hair and some teeth. Then they'd be sorry. Then they'd wail and gnash. But it would be too late.

"How could we have forgotten to buy chocolate biscuits?" Dad would sob.

"We deserve to be locked up for ever!" Mum would shriek.

"And now there's nothing left of Henry but a tooth, and it's all our fault!" they'd howl.

Humph. Serve them right.

Wait. What an idiot he was. Why should he risk **DEATH** from starvation when he knew where there was a rich stash of all sorts of **YUMMY** biscuits waiting just for him?

MOODY MARGARET'S SECRET CLUB tent was sure to be full to bursting with goodies! **Horrid Henry** hadn't raided it in ages. And so long as he was quick, no one would ever know he'd left the house.

"Go on, Henry," urged his tummy. **"FEED ME!"** **Horrid Henry** didn't need to be urged twice.

Slowly, quietly, he SNEAKED out of bed, crept down the stairs and tiptoed out of the back door. Then quick over the wall, and hey presto, he was in the Secret Club tent. There was MARGARET'S SECRET CLUB biscuit tin, in her pathetic hiding place under a blanket. HA!

Horrid Henry prised open the lid. Oh wow. It was filled to

the brim with **Chocolate Fudge Chewies!** And those scrumptious **TRIPLE CHOCOLATE CHIP MARSHMALLOW SQUIDGIES!** Henry scooped up a huge handful and stuffed them in his mouth.

CHOMP. CHOMP. CHOMP.

Oh wow. Oh wow. Was there anything more delicious in the whole wide world than a mouthful of nicked biscuits?

"**MORE! MORE! MORE!**" yelped his tummy.

Who was **Horrid Henry** to say no?

Henry reached in to snatch another mega handful . . .

BANG! SLAM! BANG! STOMP! STOMP! STOMP!

"That's too bad, Gurinder," snapped Margaret's voice. "It's my party so I decide. Hurry up, Susan."

"I am hurrying," said Susan's voice.

The footsteps were heading straight for the **SECRET CLUB** tent.

Yikes. What was Margaret doing outside at this time of night? There wasn't a moment to lose.

Horrid Henry looked around wildly. Where could he hide? There was a wicker chest at the back, where Margaret kept her dressing-up clothes. Horrid Henry *leapt* inside and pulled the lid shut. Hopefully, the girls wouldn't be long and he could escape home before Mum and Dad discovered he'd been out.

MOODY MARGARET bustled into the tent, followed by her mother, Gorgeous Gurinder, Kung-Fu Kate, Lazy Linda, Vain Violet, Singing Soraya and Sour Susan.

"Now, girls, it's late, I want you to go straight to bed, lights out, no talking," said Margaret's mother. "My little Maggie Moo Moo needs her beauty sleep."

HA, thought Horrid Henry. Margaret could sleep for a thousand

years and she'd still look like a *frog*.

"Yes, Mum," said Margaret.

"Good night, girls," trilled
Margaret's mum. "See you in the
morning."

Phew, thought Horrid Henry, lying
as still as he could. He'd be back
home in no time, mission safely
accomplished.

"We're sleeping out here?" said

Singing Soraya. "In a tent?"

"I said it was a SECRET CLUB sleepover," said Margaret.

Horrid Henry's heart **sank**. Huh? They were planning to sleep here? **RATS RATS RATS DOUBLE RATS.** He was going to have to hide inside this hot dusty chest until they were asleep.

Maybe they'll all fall asleep soon, thought Horrid Henry hopefully.

Because he had to get home before Mum and Dad discovered he was missing. If they realised he'd SNEAKED

outside, he'd be in so much trouble
his life wouldn't be worth living and
he might as well abandon all hope of
ever watching **TV** or eating another
biscuit until he was an **old, shrivelled
bag of bones** struggling to chew with
his one tooth and watch telly with
his magnifying glass and hearing aid.
Yikes!

Horrid Henry looked grimly at the

biscuits clutched in his fist. Thank goodness he'd brought provisions. He might be trapped here for a very long time.

"Where's your sleeping bag, Violet?" said Margaret.

"I didn't bring one," said Vain Violet. "I don't like sleeping on the floor."

"**Tough**," said Margaret, "that's where we're sleeping."

"But I need to sleep in a bed," whined Vain Violet. "I don't want to sleep out here."

"Well, we do," said Margaret.

"Yeah," said Susan.

"I can sleep anywhere," said Lazy Linda, yawning.

"I'm calling my mum," said Violet. **"I want to go home."**

"Go ahead," said Margaret. "We don't need you, do we?"

Silence.

"Oh go on, Violet, stay," said Gurinder.

"Yeah, stay," said Kung-Fu Kate.

"No!" said Violet, *flouncing* out of the tent.

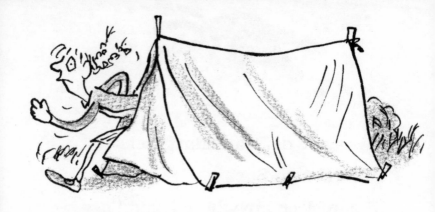

"Hummph," said Moody Margaret.
"She's no fun anyway. Now, everyone
put your sleeping bags down where I
say. I need to sleep by the entrance,
because I need fresh air."

"I want to sleep by the entrance,"
said Soraya.

"No," said Margaret, "it's my party
so I decide. Susan, you go at the back
because you snore."

"Do not," said Susan.

"Do too," said Margaret.

"Liar."

"Liar."

SLAP!

SLAP!

"That's it!" wailed Susan. "I'm calling my mum."

"Go ahead," said Margaret, "see if I care, snore-box. That'll be loads more **Chocolate Fudge Chewies** for the rest of us."

Sour Susan stood still. She'd been looking forward to Margaret's sleepover for ages. And she still hadn't had any of the **MIDNIGHT FEAST** Margaret had promised.

"All right, I'll stay," said Susan sourly, putting her sleeping bag down at the back of the tent by the dressing-up chest.

"I want to be next to Gurinder," said Lazy Linda, scratching her head.

"Do you have **NITS?**" said Gurinder.

"No!" said Linda.

"You do too," said Gurinder.

"Do not," said Linda.

"Do too," said Gurinder. "I'm not sleeping next to someone who has nits."

"Me neither," said Kate.

"Me neither," said Soraya.

"Don't look at me," said Margaret. "I'm not sleeping next to you."

"I don't have nits!" wailed Linda.

"Go next to Susan," said Margaret.

"But she snores," protested Linda.

"But she has nits," protested Susan.

"Do not."

"Do not."

"Snory!"

"NITTY!"

Suddenly something scuttled across the floor.

"EEEEK!" squealed Soraya. "It's a mouse!" She scrambled on to the dressing-up chest. The lid sagged.

"It won't hurt you," said Margaret.

"Yeah," said Susan.

"EEEEK!" squealed Linda, shrinking back.

162

The lid sagged even more.

CREE—EAAAK went the chest.

Aaarrrrggghhh, thought **Horrid Henry**, trying to squash himself down before he was squished.

"Eeeek!" squealed Gurinder, scrambling on to the chest.

CREE—EAAAAAK! went the chest.

Errrrgh, thought **Horrid Henry**,

pushing up against the sagging lid as hard as he could.

"I can't sleep if there's a . . . mouse," said Gurinder. She looked around nervously. "What if it runs on top of my sleeping bag?"

Margaret sighed. "It's only a mouse," she said.

"I'm scared of mice," whimpered Gurinder. "I'm leaving!" And she ran out of the tent, wailing.

"More food for the rest of us," said Margaret, shrugging. "I say we feast now."

"About time," said Soraya.

"Let's start with the **Chocolate Fudge Chewies**," said Margaret, opening the **SECRET CLUB** biscuit tin. "Everyone can have two, except for me, I get four 'cause it's my . . ."

Margaret peered into the tin. There were only a few crumbs inside.

"Who stole the biscuits?" said Margaret.

"Wasn't me," said Susan.

"Wasn't me," said Soraya.

"Wasn't me," said Kate.

"Wasn't me," said Linda.

TEE HEE, thought **Horrid Henry**.

"One of you did, so no one is getting anything to eat until you admit it," snapped Margaret.

"**MEANIE**," muttered Susan sourly.

"What did you say?" said Moody Margaret.

"Nothing," said Susan.

"Then we'll just have to wait for the culprit to come forward," said Margaret, scowling. "Meanwhile, get into your sleeping bags. We're going to tell *scary* stories in the dark. Who knows a good one?"

"I do," said Susan.

"Not the story about the ghost kitty-cat which drank up all the milk in your kitchen, is it?" said Margaret.

Susan scowled.

"Well, it's a true *scary* story," said Susan.

"I know a real scary story," said Kung-Fu Kate. "It's about this **MONSTER**—"

"Mine's better," said Margaret. "It's about a **flesh-eating zombie** which creeps around at night and rips off—"

"**NOoOo**," wailed Linda. "I hate being scared. I'm calling my mum to come and get me."

"No scaredy-cats allowed in the Secret Club," said Margaret.

"I don't care," said Linda, *flouncing* out.

"It's not a sleepover unless we tell **GHOST** stories," said Moody Margaret. "Turn off your torches. It won't be scary unless we're all sitting in the dark."

SNIFFLE. SNIFFLE. SNIFFLE.

"I want to go home," snivelled Soraya. "I've never slept away from home before . . . *I want my mummy.*"

"What a baby," said Moody Margaret.

Horrid Henry was cramped and hot and uncomfortable. Pins and needles were shooting up his arm. He shifted his shoulder, brushing against the lid.

There was a muffled **creak**.

Henry froze. Whoops. Henry prayed they hadn't heard anything.

". . . and the **zombie** crept inside the tent gnashing its bloody teeth and sniffing the air for human flesh, hungry for more—"

Ow. His poor aching arm. Henry shifted position again.

Creak . . .

"What was that?" whispered Susan.

"What was what?" said Margaret.

"There was a . . . a . . . creak . . ."
said Susan.

"The wind," said Margaret.
"Anyway, the zombie sneaked into
the tent and—"

"You don't think . . ." hissed Kate.

"Think what?" said Margaret.

"That the zombie . . . the zombie . . ."

I'm starving, thought Horrid Henry. I'll just eat a few biscuits really, really, really quietly—

CRUNCH. CRUNCH.

"What was that?" whispered Susan.

"What was what?" said Margaret. "You're ruining the story."

"That . . . crunching sound," hissed Susan.

Horrid Henry gasped. What an idiot he was! Why hadn't he thought of this before?

CRUNCH. CRUNCH. CRUNCH.

"Like someone . . . someone . . . crunching on . . . bones," whispered Kung-Fu Kate.

"Someone . . . here . . ." whispered Susan.

TAP. **Horrid Henry** rapped on the underside of the lid.

TAP! TAP! TAP!

"I didn't hear anything," said Margaret loudly.

"It's the **zombie!**" screamed Susan.

"He's in here!" screamed Kate. **"AAAAARRRRRRRGHHHHHHH!"**

"I'm going home!" screamed Susan and Kate. "MUMMMMMMMMMYYYY!" they wailed, running off.

Ha ha, thought **Horrid Henry**. His *brilliant* plan had worked!!! **TEE HEE**. He'd hop out, steal the rest of the feast and scoot home. Hopefully Mum and Dad—

YANK!

Suddenly the chest lid was flung open and a torch shone in his eyes. MOODY MARGARET'S hideous face *glared* down at him.

"Gotcha!" said Moody Margaret. "Oh boy, are you in trouble. Just wait till I tell on you. HA HA, Henry, you're dead."

Horrid Henry climbed out of the chest and brushed a few crumbs on to the carpet.

"Just wait till I tell everyone at school about your sleepover," said Horrid Henry. "How you were so

175

MEAN and **BOSSY** everyone ran away."

"Your parents will punish you for ever," said Moody Margaret.

"Your name will be mud for ever," said Horrid Henry. "Everyone will laugh at you and it serves you right, *Maggie Moo Moo*."

"Don't call me that," said Margaret, glaring.

"Call you what, *Moo Moo*?"

"All right," said Margaret slowly. "I won't tell on you if you give me **two** packs of **Chocolate Fudge Chewies**."

"No way," said Henry. "I won't tell on you if you give me **three** packs of **Chocolate Fudge Chewies**."

"Fine," said Margaret. "Your parents are still up. I'll tell them where you are right now. I wouldn't want them to worry."

"Go ahead," said Henry. "I can't wait until school tomorrow."

Margaret scowled.

"Just this once," said Horrid Henry. "I won't tell on you if you won't tell on me."

"Just this once," said Moody

Margaret. "But never again."

They *glared* at each other.

When he was king, thought Horrid Henry, anyone named Margaret would be catapulted over the walls into an oozy swamp. Meanwhile . . . on guard, Margaret. On guard. I will be avenged!

HORRID HENRY

AND THE MAD PROFESSOR

Horrid Henry grabbed
the top secret sweet tin
he kept hidden under his
bed. It was jam-packed with all
his favourites: **Big Boppers**. Nose
Pickers. **DIRT BALLS**. HOT SNOT.
Gooey Chewies. SCRUNCHY
MUNCHIES.

Yummy!!!

Hmmm boy! **Horrid Henry's**
mouth watered as he prised off the
lid. Which to have first? A **DIRT
BALL?** Or a **Gooey Chewy?** Actually,
he'd just scoff the lot. It had been

ages since he'd . . .

Huh?

Where were all his chocolates?
Where were all his *sweets?* Who'd
nicked them? Had Margaret invaded
his room? Had Peter sneaked in?
How dare— Oh. **Horrid Henry**
suddenly remembered. He'd eaten
them all.

RATS.
RATS.
TRIPLE RATS.

Well, he'd just have to go and buy
more. He was sure to have **LOADS**

of pocket money left.

Chocolate, here I come, thought Horrid Henry, heaving his bones and dashing over to his skeleton bank.

He shook it. Then he shook it again.

There wasn't even a rattle.

How could he have **NO MONEY** and no sweets? It was so unfair! Just last night Peter had been boasting about having £7.48 in his piggy bank. And loads of sweets left over from Hallowe'en. **Horrid Henry** scowled. Why did Peter always have money?

Why did he, Henry, never have money?

Money was totally wasted on Peter. What was the point of Peter having **POCKET MONEY** since he never spent it? Come to think of it, what was the point of Peter having *sweets* since he never ate them?

There was a shuffling, scuttling noise, then Perfect Peter dribbled into Henry's bedroom carrying all his soft toys.

"Get out of my room, **worm!**" bellowed Horrid Henry, holding his nose. "You're stinking it up."

"I am not," said Peter.

"Are too, **SMELLY PANTS**."

"I do not have smelly pants," said Peter.

"Do too, **woofy, poofy, pongy pants**."

Peter opened his mouth, then closed it.

"Henry, will you play with me?" said Peter.

"**NO**."

"Please?"

"No!"

"Pretty please?"

"No!!"

"But we could play school with all my cuddly toys," said Peter. "Or have a tea party with them . . ."

"For the last time, **NOOOOOOO!**" screamed Horrid Henry.

"You never play with me," said Perfect Peter.

"That's 'cause you're a **toad-faced nappy wibble bibble**," said Horrid Henry. "Now go away and leave me alone."

188

"Mum! Henry's calling me names again!" screamed Peter. "He called me wibble bibble."

"Henry! Don't be **HORRID!**" shouted Mum.

"I'm not being horrid, Peter's annoying me!" yelled Henry.

"Henry's annoying me!" yelled Peter. "**MAKE HIM STOP!**" screamed Henry and Peter.

Mum ran into the room.

"Boys. If you can't play nicely then leave each other alone," said Mum.

"Henry won't play with me," wailed

Peter. "He never plays with me."

"Henry! Why can't you play with your brother?" said Mum. "When I was little, Ruby and I played beautifully together all the time."

Horrid Henry **SCOWLED**.

"Because he's a ***wormy worm***," said Henry.

"Mum! Henry just called me a wormy worm," wailed Peter.

"Don't call your brother names," said Mum.

"Peter only wants to play **stupid** baby games," said Henry.

"I do not," said Peter.

"If you're not going to play together then you can do your chores," said Mum.

"I've done mine," said Peter. "I fed Fluffy, cleaned out the litter tray and tidied my room."

Mum beamed. "Peter, you are the

best boy in the world."

Horrid Henry scowled. He'd been far too busy reading his **COMICS** to empty the wastepaper bins and tidy his room. He stuck out his tongue at Peter behind Mum's back.

"Henry's making **HORRIBLE** faces at me," said Peter.

"Henry, please be nice for once and play with Peter," said Mum. She sighed and left the room.

Henry *glared* at Peter.

Peter *glared* at Henry.

Horrid Henry was about to push

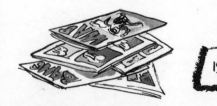

Peter out the door when suddenly he had a brilliant, SPECTACULAR idea. It was so brilliant and so SPECTACULAR that Horrid Henry couldn't believe he was still standing in his bedroom and hadn't BLASTED off into outer space trailing clouds of glory. Why had he never thought of this before? It was **MAGNIFICENT**. It was genius. One day he would start *Henry's Genius Shop*, where people would pay a million pounds to buy his **SUPER FANTASTIC** ideas. But until then...

"Okay, Peter, I'll play with you," said Horrid Henry. He smiled sweetly.

Perfect Peter could hardly believe his ears.

"You'll . . . play with me?" said Perfect Peter.

"Sure," said **Horrid Henry**.

"What do you want to play?" asked Peter cautiously. The last time Peter could remember Henry playing with him they'd played **Cannibals and Dinner**. Peter had had to be dinner . . .

"Let's play **Robot and Mad Professor**," said Henry.

"Okay," said Perfect Peter. Wow. That sounded a lot more exciting than his usual favourite game — writing lists of vegetables or having ladybird tea parties with his stuffed toys. He'd probably have to be the robot and do what Henry said, but it would be worth it, to play such a fun game.

"I'll be the robot," said Horrid Henry.

Peter's jaw dropped.

"Go on," said Henry. "You're the mad professor. Tell me what to do."

WOW. Henry was even letting him be the **mad professor**. Maybe he'd been wrong about Henry . . . maybe Henry had been struck by lightning and changed into a nice brother . . .

"Robot," ordered Perfect Peter. "March around the room."

Horrid Henry didn't budge.

"Robot!" said Peter. "I order you to march."

"Pro—fes—sor! I—need—twenty-five—p—to—move," said Henry in a robotic voice. "Twenty-five p. Twenty-

five p. Twenty-five p."

"Twenty-five p?" said Peter.

"That's the rules of **Robot and Mad Professor**," said Henry, shrugging.

"Okay, Henry," said Peter, rummaging in his bank. He handed Henry 25p.

Yes! thought **Horrid Henry**.

Horrid Henry took a few stiff steps, then slowed down and stopped.

"More," said robotic Henry. "More. My batteries have run down. More."

Perfect Peter handed over another 25p.

Henry *lurched* around for a few more steps, **crashed** into the wall and collapsed on the floor.

"I need sweets to get up," said the robot. "Fetch me sweets. Systems overload. Sweets. Sweets. Sweets."

Perfect Peter dropped two sweets into Henry's hand. Henry twitched his foot.

"More," said the robot. "Lots more."

Perfect Peter dropped four more sweets. Henry jerked up into a sitting position.

"I will now tell you my top secret—secret—secret—secret—" stuttered **Horrid Henry**. "Cross—my—palm—with—silver and sweets . . ." He held out his robot hand. Peter filled it.

TEE HEE.

"I want to be the robot now," said Peter.

"Okay, robot," said Henry. "Run upstairs and empty all the waste-paper baskets. Bet you can't do it in thirty seconds."

"Yes I can," said Peter.

"Nah, you're too **rusty** and PUNY," said Horrid Henry.

"Am not," said Peter.

"Then prove it, robot," said Henry.

"But aren't you going to give me—" faltered Peter.

"**MOVE!**" bellowed Henry. "They don't call me the *MAD* professor for nothing!!!"

Playing *Robot and Mad Professor* was a bit less fun than Peter had anticipated. Somehow, his piggy bank was now empty and Henry's skeleton bank was full. And somehow most of Peter's Hallowe'en sweets were now in Henry's sweet box.

Robot and Mad Professor was the most **FUN** Henry had ever had

playing with Peter. Now that he had all Peter's money and all Peter's sweets, could he trick Peter into doing all his chores as well?

"Let's play school," said Peter. That would be safe. There was no way Henry could trick him playing that . . .

"I've got a better idea," said Henry. "Let's play BUTLERS AND GENTLEMEN. You're the butler. I order you to . . ."

"No," interrupted Peter. "I don't want to." Henry couldn't make him.

"Okay," said Henry. "We can play school. You can be the tidy monitor."

Oh! Peter loved being tidy monitor.

"We're going to play Clean Up
the Classroom!" said Henry. "The
classroom is in here. So, get to work."

Peter looked around at the
great mess of TOYS and DIRTY
CLOTHES and COMICS and empty
wrappers scattered all over Henry's
room.

"I thought we'd start by taking the

register," said Peter.

"Nah," said Henry. "That's the baby way to play school. You have to start by tidying the classroom. You're the tidy monitor."

"What are you?" said Peter.

"The teacher, of course," said Henry.

"Can I be the teacher next?" said Peter.

"Sure," said Henry. "We'll swap after you finish your job."

Henry lay on his bed and read his COMIC and stuffed the rest of Peter's sweets into his mouth. Peter tidied.

Ah, this was the life.

"It's very quiet in here," said Mum, popping her head round the door. "What's going on?"

"Nothing," said Horrid Henry.

"Why is Peter tidying your room?" said Mum.

"'Cause he's the tidy monitor," said Henry.

Perfect Peter burst into tears. "Henry's taken all my money and all my sweets and made me do all his chores," he wailed.

"**HENRY!**" shouted Mum. "**YOU HORRID BOY!**"

On the bad side, Mum made Henry give Peter back all his money. But on the good side, all his chores were done for the week. And he couldn't give Peter back his sweets because he'd eaten them all.

Result!

HORRID HENRY

RAINY DAY DISASTER!

Turn the
page for some
DISASTROUSLY
fun bonus games
and activities!

Adult supervision is
recommended when glue,
scissors and other sharp
points are in use

Make Your own Grisly Grub Box

THERE'S NOTHING HORRID HENRY LIKES BETTER ON A RAINY DAY THAN SNEAKING A FEW TREATS OUT OF HIS GRISLY GRUB BOX!

You will need:

1 cardboard box with a lid

1 glue stick

1 pair of scissors - ask an adult for help cutting!

wrapping paper or any old newspapers

Your favourite pens & pencils

MAKE YOUR OWN GRISLY GRUB BOX WITH THESE 6 EASY STEPS!

1. Find an old cardboard box with a lid. It should be about the size of a shoebox. Take the lid off.

2. Grab a roll of wrapping paper (or an old newspaper) and wrap it around the box, using your glue to stick it down.

3. Now wrap and glue the lid of the box.

4. Take a black pen or pencil and draw a skull and crossbones on the lid of the box.

5. Now decorate your box with any drawings, stickers or other decorations you'd like.

6. The BEST part! Fill your grub box with all your favourite treats (ask an adult for permission first).

Moody Margaret's Maze

MOODY MARGARET LOVES TO TRICK HORRID HENRY SO SHE'S DRAWN HIM A REALLY DIFFICULT MAZE. HELP HENRY COMPLETE THE MAZE BY FINDING THE SWEETS.

START

Rude Ralph's Wisecracks

RUDE RALPH IS TRYING OUT SOME NEW RUDE JOKES.
WHICH JOKE IS YOUR FAVOURITE?

1. WHAT HAPPENED TO THE FLY ON THE TOILET SEAT?
   It got peed-off.

2. WHAT COMES OUT OF YOUR NOSE AT 150 MILES PER HOUR?
   A lambogreeny.

3. WHAT'S BROWN AND STICKY?
   A stick.

4. WHY DID THE TOILET PAPER ROLL DOWN THE HILL?
   To get to the bottom.

5. WHAT DOES A CLOUD WEAR?
   Thunderwear.

6. WHY DIDN'T THE SKELETON CROSS THE ROAD?
   He didn't have the guts to do it!

7. WHAT DO YOU CALL A STRAWBERRY WHO IS SAD?
   A blueberry!

8. WHAT COLOUR IS A BURP?
   Burple!

Rainy Day Drawing

HORRID HENRY FINDS RAINY DAYS SO BORING! LUCKILY HE'S GOT THIS FUN DRAWING GAME TO PLAY WITH HIS FRIENDS.

- Fold a piece of paper into four.
- The first person draws their favourite character's head at the top of the page.
- Fold the paper over to hide the head and pass it to a friend to draw the upper body.
- Keep going in the same way, adding legs and feet.
- Unravel the paper and see who you've drawn. Did you all draw the same character or have you got a funny new character?

Invasion Wordsearch

PERFECT PETER HATES IT WHEN HENRY INVADES HIS BEDROOM. CAN YOU FIND TEN WORDS ABOUT HENRY'S ROOM INVASION IN THE CROSSWORD BELOW?

SHEEP · PETER · HENRY · FROGFACE · SKULLBANGER · SABOTAGE · BUNNYKINS · INVASION · BURGLAR · THIEF

G	G	Q	X	S	R	Y	Z	P	A	L	V	P	L	H
T	M	F	M	Y	N	T	D	J	G	B	I	H	T	U
D	S	H	S	B	T	I	Z	F	B	V	W	T	H	X
H	B	K	X	Y	V	L	K	A	E	Z	T	J	I	L
Y	E	I	I	T	Y	D	E	Y	K	Y	V	Y	E	K
N	S	A	B	O	T	A	G	E	N	R	M	D	F	Z
O	M	S	W	B	O	F	P	L	R	N	O	C	Y	E
I	Y	W	R	J	S	H	E	E	P	E	U	M	Q	O
S	Y	P	E	T	E	R	B	E	M	H	T	B	N	P
A	J	M	C	S	K	U	L	L	B	A	N	G	E	R
V	N	U	H	Z	W	M	C	O	S	F	M	S	W	A
N	W	E	C	A	F	G	O	R	F	T	F	X	N	T
I	F	X	F	T	M	W	Q	D	B	B	R	S	T	Y
N	C	X	B	F	D	Y	C	R	A	L	G	R	U	B
H	D	N	I	P	Y	D	R	I	O	G	Y	U	U	P

Moody Margaret's Sleepover checklist

MOODY MARGARET ALWAYS LIKES TO BE PREPARED
WHEN PLANNING HER SLEEPOVERS. USE HER
CHECKLIST TO PLAN YOUR NEXT SLEEPOVER.

WHO ARE YOU INVITING?

1. Sour Susan ○
2. Vain Violet ○
3. Horrid Henry ○

WHAT'S THE THEME?

1. A Gross-out slime party! ○
2. Daffy and her Dancing Daisies flower party! ○
3. Rapper Zapper dance party! ○

WHAT'S ON THE MENU?

1. Triple chocolate chip marshmallow squidgies! ○
2. Pizza and lots of chips! ○
3. Homemade burgers and salad ○

WHICH GAMES ARE YOU PLAYING?

1. Hide-and-seek until we're tired ◯
2. We're building a massive pillow fort! ◯
3. All our favourite board games ◯

YOU'RE GOING TO WATCH . . .

1. An action movie ◯
2. A scary movie of course! ◯
3. Something funny ◯

WHERE ARE YOU GOING TO SLEEP?

1. In the Secret club tent ◯
2. In the fort we built earlier ◯
3. Curled up in our sleeping bags
   in the living room ◯

AT MIDNIGHT YOU'LL BE . . .

1. Raiding the biscuit tin! ◯
2. Telling ghost stories - spooky! ◯
3. Asleep! It's way past my bedtime ◯

Sour Susan's Spot the Difference

SOUR SUSAN IS MARGARET'S BEST FRIEND BUT THEY DON'T ALWAYS GET ALONG. SPOT THE SIX DIFFERENCES IN THE PICTURE ON THE RIGHT.

Super Sudoku

HORRID HENRY IS STUCK ON THIS TRICKY SUDOKU PUZZLE.
CAN YOU HELP HIM SOLVE IT?

4	2			5	1	3		9
		8	3	4				
6	3	5	9	7		8		
	4	3		2	5	7	9	6
		2			8	4	1	
		6		3	4			8
	6		5	8	3		7	
3		4	2		9	1	8	5
	8		4	1	7	6	3	2

Weepy William's Would You Rather

WEEPY WILLIAM HAS SOME QUESTIONS FOR YOU!

1. WOULD YOU RATHER BE ABLE TO TALK TO ANIMALS OR READ PEOPLE'S MINDS?

2. WOULD YOU RATHER HAVE TO DRINK EVERYTHING FROM YOUR EARS OR EAT EVERYTHING THROUGH YOUR BELLY BUTTON?

3. WOULD YOU RATHER HAVE TO FIGHT 100 PIGEON-SIZED ZEBRAS OR ONE ZEBRA-SIZED PIGEON?

4. WOULD YOU RATHER ALWAYS NEED TO SHOUT WHENEVER YOU SPEAK OR ALWAYS HAVE TO WHISPER?

5. WOULD YOU RATHER GET CAUGHT FARTING OR PICKING YOUR NOSE?

6. WOULD YOU RATHER ONLY EAT FOODS THAT LOOK DISGUSTING OR SMELL DISGUSTING?

7. WOULD YOU RATHER STICK YOUR HANDS IN A BOWL OF EYEBALLS OR A BOWL OF BRAINS?

8. WOULD YOU RATHER BE ABLE TO SPEAK EVERY LANGUAGE ON EARTH OR COMMUNICATE WITH ALIENS?

9. WOULD YOU RATHER HAVE ALL THE FOOD YOU EVER WANTED OR HAVE ALL THE TOYS YOU EVER WANTED?

10. WOULD YOU RATHER NEVER HAVE HOMEWORK AGAIN OR NEVER TAKE A TEST AGAIN?